The Glo Friends live in a magical place called Glo Land. This colourful rhyming story tells of one of their adventures.

British Library Cataloguing in Publication Data
Woodman, June
    Glo Cricket.—(Glo friends; 1)
    I. Title   II. Layfield, Kathie   III. Series
    823'.914[J]   PZ7
    ISBN 0-7214-0979-2

First edition
Published by Ladybird Books Ltd Loughborough Leicestershire UK
Ladybird Books Inc Lewiston Maine 04240 USA

GLO Friends™

GLO Cricket's merry chase

written by JUNE WOODMAN
illustrated by KATHIE LAYFIELD

Ladybird Books

Glo Cricket is a lively bug
Who hates things to go wrong.
She loves to sing, and play all kinds
Of music, all day long.

Of all the many Glo Land friends
No one can jump so high.
She *has* been heard to boast that she
Can nearly reach the sky.

But though she's really rather vain,
At heart she's very kind.
The Glo Friends say a better friend
Would be quite hard to find.

One night as she is playing some
Of her sweet lullabies,
She sees a shower of Moondrops fall
Down from the summer skies.

The others must be sleeping, for
They certainly don't see.
"I'll get the drops myself," she thinks.
"How clever that will be!"

So swiftly through the scented night
She runs beneath the moon;
She takes a bucket for the drops
That she will gather soon.

But just where *have* they fallen?
She was sure that she could tell.
The woods are dark and silent as
Though underneath a spell.

Glo Cricket sings a little song to
Keep her spirits high.
Her voice gets very quavery
And ends up with a sigh.

She's feeling very lonely and
She's feeling gloomy too.
Those Moondrops are so hard to find –
Now what is she to do?

The prickly brambles scratch her as
She searches by the stream.
Then clinging vine roots trip her up,
It's just like a bad dream.

Next, with a splash, she's fallen in.
The water's cold and deep.
Glo Cricket wishes she were home
In bed, and fast asleep.

She clambers out all cold and wet,
"I'll try another way.
I *will* find those new Moondrops if
It takes till break of day!"

She pushes through the undergrowth
And jumps a fallen tree,
But then lands in some nettles. It's
Too dark for her to see.

"Because I'm cold and lonely my
Glow's fading, I expect.
But I'm determined I shan't fail,
Those drops I will collect!"

So urging herself onward, she
Is sure she'll reach her goal.
But just as she feels better she
Falls down a rabbit hole!

Oh, what a dreadful shock she gets
As she lands with a thud.
First tripped, then wet, then stung, she's now
Knee-deep in sticky mud!

The rabbit hole is not too deep
For her to clamber out.
She thinks, "What an adventure
To tell all my friends about!"

While resting on a fallen log
She hears a well-known sound.
Some Moligans are on the march!
But she must *not* be found.

With one huge hop and one great jump
She leaps into a tree.
Now surely she'll be nice and safe
Up there – no one will see.

"But what about my glow?" she gasps.
"It really would be best
If I could be *quite* hidden." Then
She finds an old crow's nest.

She gets inside, and wriggles down
Till no glow can be seen.
The nest is soft and warm, but it
Can hardly be called clean.

Glo Cricket lies all safe and snug
And listens to the sounds
Of noisy bangs and crashes, as
The Moligans look round.

The Moligans start moaning.
"It isn't fair!" they say.
"We're tired, for we search all night,
Then dig for gold all day."

"We must just look harder,
And catch those Glo Friends bright.
Then our mine will be well-lit, and
We can sleep at night!"

Glo Cricket crouches lower as
She overhears them plan
To go on searching all that night –
She'll stop them – if she can!

So with a sudden shriek she jumps
Quite lightly from the tree.
As their leader hears the noise, he turns –
"Hey! Look what I can see!"

"A Glo Friend!" yell the Moligans,
All grinning with delight.
"Come on, we'll catch her easily,
Then our mine will be light."

They race after Glo Cricket, who
Leads them a merry chase.
The Moligans are panting, for
She jumps at such a pace.

Now cunningly Glo Cricket lures
Them to the rabbit place;
One twists his ankle, trips the rest –
And then lands on his face.

But scrambling up, they stagger on,
They're making such a din.
Glo Cricket jumps the nettle patch –
The Moligans fall in!

Glo Cricket leaps the stream and lands
Upon the other side.
She slips into the bushes where
It's dark and safe to hide.

Then how she giggles as she sees
The Moligans all crash
Straight down the bank beside the stream,
And fall in with a SPLASH!

They're all too busy quarrelling
To see her creep away.
At last her luck has changed, because
Dark night has turned to day.

Quite close beside her she can see
Moondrops caught in the flowers.
She tips them in her bucket which
She's held onto for *hours!*

Now she's safely home again
With Glo Friends crowding round.
"Oh, you are *clever*," they all cry,
"Just look what you have found!"

Glo Cricket modestly declares
That it was easy – though
Glo Grannybug sees she's a mess and
To bed she has to go!

But all admiring Glo Friends say
She's quite the brightest miss.
Glo Grannybug says she deserves
A hug, and a big kiss!